Maze Runner Parody – The Dazed Runner

By The Parody Brothers

Original Illustrations created by Online Monkeys
www.onlinemonkeys.com.au

Other books by the Parody Brothers:

Fifty Shades of Plaid: A Choose Your Own Parody Based on E L James Most Excellent Erotic Novel

Blood Feud! It's the Clintons Vs. the Obamas for the Iron Throne!

Disclaimer

This document is geared towards providing exact and reliable information in regards to the topic and issue covered. The publication is sold with the idea that the publisher is not required to render accounting, officially permitted, or otherwise, qualified services. If advice is necessary, legal or professional, a practiced individual in the profession should be ordered.

- From a Declaration of Principles which was accepted and approved equally by a Committee of the American Bar Association and a Committee of Publishers and Associations.

The information provided herein is stated to be truthful and consistent, in that any liability, in terms of inattention or otherwise, by any usage or abuse of any policies, processes, or directions contained within is the solitary and utter responsibility of the recipient reader. Under no circumstances will any legal responsibility or blame be held against the publisher for any reparation, damages, or monetary loss due to the information herein, either directly or indirectly.

Table Of Contents

An Introduction To The Dazed Runner

NOTE: There are spoilers below. Although we assume you have read The Maze Runner already, on the off chance you haven't, go read it first! It is a good book and you'll appreciate this parody much more for having done so. If you have read the book please proceed. Just don't complain to us that you weren't warned!

What you are about to read is our graphic novel parody of James Dashner's The Maze Runner. This immensely popular book, which has just recently been made into a successful movie, is the latest example of the young adult dystopian novel. Whether it is The Hunger Games, Divergent, or the Maze Runner the basic premise of these books remains the same. A young hero just on the edge of adult hood is forced to fight an oppressive system of some kind.

Did we enjoy the book? We actually did! However, although the book was definitely a page-turner there were just some things about it that were beyond belief. Forget about the giant maze, how about just the idea that a group of teenage boys could work together? Has the author ever met a teenage boy in his life? Or the idea that all of these boys are so smart yet none of these little Einstein's could figure out what WICKED stood for? And what about the whole idea behind The Maze itself? If it was created as a test to weed out the weakest boys in a survival of the fittest kind of way, why were the deaths so random? It just doesn't make any sense!

Of course, even the vaunted Hunger Games didn't make that much sense either. Would a totalitarian government really create a contest where the children of the districts are forced to fight to the death? Wouldn't this be more likely to ignite a rebellion than not? Like the Maze Runner, The Hunger Game's main story doesn't make that much sense. As an allegory for a person's journey from childhood to adulthood though it works very well. The Hunger Games themselves, from our point of view, were really an allegory for the blood sport that is high school. Think about it. As a child you are thrown into this environment by adults in which there are no rules. In this environment having money matters, being attractive matters. You form cliques with like-minded people who are often allayed against other groups. It can be brutal.

The same thing goes for Maze Runner, which only makes sense as an allegory for travelling from childhood to young adulthood. Like a baby the Maze Runner characters enter the world with no conception of how they got there or where they are. The only thing they are given is a name. In the protected home of The Maze they are given tasks to perform and rules to follow as they begin to figure out the world around them. However, with the arrival of puberty (signaled by the arrival of Teresa) the adult world beckons beyond the Maze. Like the adult world The Maze offers the promise of escape yet it is also a fearful place full of danger in which the rules of home (or The Glade) do not apply.

Whoa! We didn't mean to get so serious with you so quickly! It's just that in our view to create a good parody you need to understand the book from the inside out. In The Maze Runner's case it's the space between its main nonsensical story and its underlying allegory of growing up that the parody can be found. And with that I think we've blabbed on enough. We both sincerely hope you enjoy our graphic novel parody of The Maze Runner

OUR STORY BEGINS WITH OUR HERO, THOMAS, RIDING A DARK ELEVATOR TO THE SURFACE. HE FINDS HIMSELF IN A MYSTERIOUS PLACE CALLED "THE GLADE" WHICH IS POPULATED BY A NUMBER OF TEENAGE BOYS. HE HAS NO MEMORY OF HOW HE GOT THERE. HE ALSO SOON LEARNS THAT HIS MEMORY IS NOT THE ONLY THING HE DOESN'T HAVE ...

10

As he journeyed throughout the Glade Thomas found it very hard to get a straight answer from anyone. He had a million questions about this new world he was in, but no one seemed willing to talk to him. Thankfully, a helpful stranger appeared with an explanation.

16

CHUCK AND THOMAS'S CONVERSATION IS INTERRUPTED BY THE SOUND OF A SIREN THAT HERALDS THE ARRIVAL OF THE BOX. WHO COULD BE IN IT? I CAN'T WAIT TO FIND OUT!

Minho and Alby enter the maze in order to investigate the dead Griever. When they are late though everyone is worried as they may be trapped in the Maze! However, just as the Maze starts to close Minho appears, attempting to carry a badly wounded Alby. There is no way they'll be able to get out in time! Despite there being no way for him to help them Thomas runs into the maze for seemingly no reason ... or was there?

Thomas is able to save Alby by hanging him in some vines. However he's not out of danger as both he and Minho are chased by Grievers!

Thomas and Minho are able to evade the Grievers and proceed to rescue a not too happy Alby ...

Free of the Maze a gathering is held to debate what should be done with Thomas and his flagrant breaking of the rules.

MEANWHILE ALBY STARTS TO UNDERGO THE CHANGE FROM HIS GRIEVER BITES. HE STARTS TO REMEMBER THINGS FROM HIS PAST THAT HE WANTS TO TELL THOMAS. AT LEAST THAT'S WHAT HE SAYS ...

FRUSTRATED AT THE BOYS LACK OF PROGRESS KATNISS LEADS THOMAS AND MINHO INTO THE MAZE TO FIND A WAY OUT. WHILE THERE SHE MAKES A SHOCKING DISCOVERY ....

KATNISS AND THOMAS TRY AND RALLY THE GLIDERS TO MAKE FOR THE GRIEVER HOLE. ALBY, HOWEVER, TRIES TO STOP THEM.

LED BY THOMAS AND KATNISS THE REST OF THE GLADERS MAKE IT BY ALBY TO THE GRIEVER HOLE. THERE IS AN ENORMOUS FIGHT BETWEEN THE GLADERS AND THE GRIEVERS WHICH YOU WOULD BE AMAZED AT IF YOU COULD SEE IT. THINK LORD OF THE RINGS BUT ONLY BETTER. AT ANY RATE THOMAS, KATNISS AND CHUCK MAKE IT THROUGH THE HOLE WHERE THEY FIND A COMPUTER. IF ONLY THEY CAN ENTER IN THE RIGHT CODE THEY'LL BE ABLE TO SHUT DOWN THE MAZE AND ESCAPE! CAN THEY DO IT IN TIME?

BEFORE THE GLADERS CAN CELEBRATE THEIR VICTORY A MYSTERIOUS FEMALE SCIENTIST ENTERS THE ROOM FOLLOWED BY ... GALLY?

44

BEFORE THOMAS CAN RESPOND, HOWEVER, ARMED GUNMAN BURST INTO THE ROOM, KILLING THE SCIENTIST. WHAT COULD BE THEIR MOTIVE?

About The Author

The Parody Brothers got their start writing when they lost a bet and were forced to read the book Fifty Shades Of Grey. In an attempt to come to terms with the mental scarring this caused them (Shades being a book no man was meant to read) they decided to write the parody Fifty Shades Of Plaid. They found this exercise to be so therapeutic and enjoyable they decided to write another one, which is the book you've just read. What's next for the brothers? Only time will tell.

About The Illustrator

Online Monkeys is a Web Marketing and Web/Graphic Design agency. We are at the forefront of the technological revolution and we are helping businesses to connect with the broader world via social media, mobile apps, etc. We endeavour to help businesses capitalize on the vast potential that has been unlocked by the emergence of mobile devices such as tablets, smart phones, smart watches, etc. Our team is made up of talented and creative individuals with an enormous amount of experience in business and web design. Whatever you're looking for, social media training, mobile app development, logo and caricature design and online marketing ; you name it,

http://www.onlinemonkeys.com.au/

One Last Thing

Thank you again for purchasing our book!

I hope you found our take on The Maze Runner to be amusing at the very least.

Finally, if you enjoyed this book we would both like to ask a favor of you. Would you be so kind as to leave a review for our book on Amazon or wherever you purchased it from? It would be greatly appreciated!

Thank you!

Manufactured by Amazon.ca
Bolton, ON

26686345R00031